D1794875

J. K. MEYERS

KAMA SUTRA

for Christians

My Ten Favorite Sexual Adventures

authorHOUSE®

AuthorHouse™
1663 Liberty Drive
Bloomington, IN 47403
www.authorhouse.com
Phone: 833-262-8899

Published by AuthorHouse 02/04/2021

ISBN: 978-1-6655-1608-2 (sc)
ISBN: 978-1-6655-1607-5 (e)

Library of Congress Control Number: 2021902477

Prologue

This is a very important book for all women and men no matter where their faith originates from. Sex, for centuries, has often been thought of as bad or sinful but it's not. Sex is common biology; every creature on earth has sex. Why is it only sinful when humans have sex? Throughout history there have been sects of people that taught and preached to their followers that they must stop having sex. Obviously, those sects died off.

The reason I'm writing this book is because there really are no true Christian books on the subject of sex out there. As a Christian, all my life I've been told sex is dirty or wrong—I've been lied to throughout my adult life on the subject. I've been told oral sex is wrong and anal sex is an abomination. *Newsflash*, it's not.

Here's another newsflash for you: having a wild sex life with your partner will not lead to pedophilia, as I have been told it might. Pedophilia is a crime and those sick bitches and bastards need to be taken out of society. You never see a grown lion pounce on a young lioness just to get his jollies off. It goes against nature itself for sex not to be with two mature individuals. So when sex is mentioned in this book it is always be between consenting adults. Anything else is criminal, and criminals need to pay for their crime.

I remember my first sexual experience (as I'm sure we all do—not mine but yours), and a mind-blowing sexual euphoria it was not. I even asked my mom about her first sexual experience and she said, "I just lay there and let him do his thing."

I'm thinking, *There has to be more to it than just lying there and letting him "do his thing." What about my thing?*

I grew up in Philadelphia, Pennsylvania, and the city of brotherly love it's not. We became famous for booing Santa Claus! What kind of decent city boos Santa Claus? I was a good daughter—I didn't stay out too late, didn't party like the other kids; never smoked, drank, or did drugs. I might not have been the smartest kid in class, but I sure wasn't the dumbest.

I met my first "love" at an evangelical seminar. His name was David, but he went by Davy. He said he was twenty-five, and I guess he wanted to keep his youthful swagger by having his name sound as youthful as possible. Davy said all the right things to a young and impressionable girl like me, and I was hooked. I was so in love with Davy; I believed he hung the moon in my life. I gave myself to this man over and over again.

The first time might not have been the best, but it got better the more we did it. I guess, as the saying goes, practice makes perfect. He was my first for everything—I gave him my virginity in all three places. He tasted me and couldn't get enough of my flaming pussy. I found out you can climax several different ways. My favorite and easiest was orally, but my most explosive orgasms were anally. When he rubbed my clit as he was stroking his thick penis into my ass I saw stars. Multiple orgasms actually do exist—thank you, God.

We made love in bed, in the shower—nothing was off limits or out of bounds for us. The many different places were just dangerous enough to get us both off quickly so we wouldn't get caught. I was lucky because no meant no. If I didn't want to do something, he respected me enough not to go there. We were inseparable in mind, body, and spirit. Our sex life was like the food of the gods. It maintained us throughout the day until we saw each other the next time. We had quickies and then longies(?). We were never out of reach from each other for too long. He would run out of town now and then to take care of evangelical business but was never gone for an extended time. We always found our way back into each other's arms as soon as we could. This was not just a one-sided relationship. He adored me as much as I did him. We knew this was going to last forever—forever and a day.

Then nature took over. I became so enthralled by being the center of Davy's universe and giving myself over and over to him that I might have forgotten to take my birth control pill once or twice. *Boom*, wouldn't you know it? I thought I was pregnant. But what was the worst that could happen? We had given ourselves to each other, we loved each other, and by God we would raise this child in that love.

My life crashed down upon me as reality reared its ugly head, and I found out that my "Davy" was really thirty-three and had a wife and daughter at home. How could our love have been such a lie? I'm not a homewrecker! What was I supposed to do? I kept asking myself that question over and over again.

Being a good Catholic girl, abortion was never an option, and I didn't want to stay in Philadelphia looking like a blimp and embarrassing my family. Should I say I was raped, but I'm keeping the baby? My world was spinning out of control, so I did what any sane almost-twenty-year-old girl would do. I found me a job in Miami, Florida and moved there pronto.

Before I left Philadelphia, I found out I was not pregnant. But let me tell you, false pregnancies are for real! Miami was a world away from Philadelphia, it made my red hair shinier and, I swear, my boobs bigger. The atmosphere was so much lighter, so much sunnier than dreary Philadelphia. They call Florida the "Sunshine State" for a good reason you know.

My job paid for me to continue my college education,

and I met so many different people from all walks of life. My sex life expanded as well. I had to wrestle with the fact I was not in love with most of my partners. Did that make the sex I was having wrong? No, sex is pure biology. You need to have sex just as much as you need to eat, shower, or go to the bathroom. Sometimes the sex turned into love making and sometimes it was just sex. But at all times, it was pretty damn good.

So I'm writing this book to let all the readers know sex is supposed to be fantastic. It's not dirty or to be taken for granted. Sex is a gift from God, and while we should thank God for this gift, I'm sure he doesn't want to be invited into our beds by someone saying, "Oh God, oh God, oh God, I'm about to cum!" He already knows this is happening; he's God, you know.

As you will notice, there is a background theme to these memories: that torrid lovemaking is not just for the bed. It can happen anywhere and everywhere. As long as you respect the area where you play, everything should be okay. While getting caught adds to the thrill of it all, you don't want to be caught by a child at any time. So use careful consideration of your surroundings, and you can always have a lot of fun.

This book will show you only a glimpse of the many different sexual positions there are. There are hundreds if not thousands of sexual positions, and I have picked my ten favorite ones that are fun and intense and should really get your engine running at full speed. Please, if you are going to read this book naked, be at home and, better yet, be with someone you want to have sex with. Enjoy, *mon ami.*

Foreword
by
Rev. Willie Graham

Hello, my Christian brothers and sisters. In this age of unmitigated sin, it is nice to have a book that will guide us away from that sin. Say hallelujah!

As you already know, sin has been with us since before the fall of man. This book is to set the record straight. We've been taught that sex between two consenting adults is wrong, but while in some cases that might be true, it is not in all.

This is a book for Christians that will let them blow the top off their sex lives. A sex life between two Christians should not be boring or limited to one or two sexual positions, such as missionary. God created us naked, and we only wore clothes after we became ashamed of our nakedness. When we go on to our next phase of life, when our savior comes back for us, we will start this new age just as naked as we started our last age of consciousness. We will be naked because there will be no shame in our dress or actions. Amen, preacher man! Say it like you believe it!

Sex is something that charges our batteries and gives us the energy to continue to give all of ourselves to a particular task. I believe, brothers and sisters, that the tasks handed to us will be to praise God. All our needs will be taken care of. There will be no need for farmers or architects, as we will all eat from the tree of life and will live in a mansion. Our praising to the Lord will be like a battery that will give God sustenance—he will feed upon our praises. What better way to charge our batteries than sex? Give me another amen!

We won't be robots—we will require food and sleep and sex. But, my brothers and sisters, gone from the sex will be the lust, the sin of wanting someone else. We will love together in the purest light. Sex is not dirty and is a much-needed activity that allows us to be at our peak—not just for us but for the Lord our God. Say hallelujah, my children!

Chapter 1

HE INVITED ME BACK
TO HIS PAD

I'VE BECOME QUITE EXPERIENCED SINCE my "cumming of age" in Philadelphia. One of my earliest experiences was right after my time with Davy, actually.

I pulled up next to this guy at a railroad stop; I thought he was superhot. He had long blonde hair, broad shoulders, and big hands that gripped his steering wheel. *Winner, winner, chicken dinner*, I thought.

I yelled, "Hey! Hey, I'm talking to you, cutie."

His mind must have been a million miles away as he looked in the back seat of his car to see who I was talking to and then hooked his thumb back at himself, mouthing the word "Me?"

"You're cute! Take me out to dinner tonight!" I told him. My two girlfriends in the car thought I was crazy.

Not wanting to get burned twice in a row I asked him, "You're not married, are you?" He held up his left hand and there was no ring, so I checked that off his list.

I asked him how tall he was and he responded, "Six

foot four, and I can cook pretty darn good also." I smiled a big sexy smile as I gave him my address and told him to pick me up around eightish.

We had a great supper at Red Lobster. He was so funny that he was making me rethink my decision to move to Miami. I asked him about his life, and he said he was a dangerous goods specialist at Federal Express, a karate teacher in two neighboring towns east of the city, and a bouncer at an upscale bar called Horse Feathers on the southern end of town. I asked him how horses had feathers. He laughed and said he had no idea.

After a scrumptious dinner we went to the mall and did some shopping (I had to buy a birthday present for my young nephew) after which he suggested we go back to his pad. Then he kissed me, and I knew it was on. This man knew how to kiss—he literally took my breath away. He nibbled on my lower lip as he flicked his tongue expertly across and into my mouth, just teasing me. He knew how to get my juices flowing that's for sure. Miami was looking farther and farther away.

We couldn't get back to his place quickly enough. My hands rubbed and explored, and boy, did I like what I was finding! Since it was well past 10:00 p.m. the traffic had really thinned out. We pulled into a little community center on the posh, east side of town. We got out of the car, and as he was unlocking the doors he said, "Welcome to my pad." He flipped on some auxiliary lights that lit up the room just a bit, and in the middle of the room was this ginormous gymnastic-looking pad. "This is where I teach karate," he said as he kissed me again, and we both fell on the pad.

"You kiss so great," he said as his hands were now traveling up and down my dress. "Your skin is so smooth." I'm not sure how long it took, an hour or just a few short minutes, but we were naked and loving every minute of it. He kept talking about how smooth my skin was in-between kissing and nibbling my neck, shoulders, and breasts. He was heading due south when we rolled on the pad and I found myself sitting on his face. We had just eaten a wonderful meal, but this man was attacking me like he hadn't been fed in days.

He stuck two of his big fingers inside me and had his pinky finger teasing my asshole. All the while he was sucking on my clit as I was drowning him in my juices. Between his slurps and fingering thrusts, he was telling me how he was going to treat me like a buffet and boy was he going to town! I must have cum at least three times before coming (or is it cumming) to my senses—I didn't want to be the only one receiving pleasure. When I spied his thick cock waving back and forth at me, I dove forward into a sixty-nine position and gobbled him up as quickly as I could. Dessert was served, and it was a heaping helping of man meat!

We were so hungry for each other—he put me on my

knees, slipping his cock into my very wet pussy. "Hold on, cowboy," I panted. "I haven't had someone of your size in me before, so take it slowly. Don't want to rip my v-jay jay wide open."

"Oh, come on now, I'm not that big. Just above average, or so I've been told," he quipped as he slid all the way inside me.

"Don't know who you've been with, but there is nothing average about that cock. This must be what giving birth is like," I moaned. He had both my arms by the wrist as he was pumping away from behind, doggy style.

We fucked back and forth in a bunch of different positions for a good thirty minutes as our tongues dueled in each other's mouths. I asked him when was he going to cum.

"Anytime you're ready for me to cum, darling," he panted and moaned.

"Oh, I'm so ready, if you … don't cum … inside me," I hoarsely panted, "I … think … I'm … about … to … *diiiieeeee!*"

I should have said that fifteen minutes ago because then he said, "I'm about to cum, darling," and *boom*—it happened. It was so hot that it actually burned my insides. There was no escape as he let out a roar that mixed with my screams of delight. I was pretty sure anyone driving by could have heard us. This man was a superman! No shrinkage here—after dumping about a pint of that hot gooey nectar in me, he was still hard! In one smooth move he rolled me on my back and pushed my knees to my shoulders. My legs scissored around his waist and he kept thrusting inside me. I came so many times that I lost count, but I'm sure it broke my personal record. I was well into the double digits before I lost count.

A sheen of sweat coated our bodies as we lay on the big gymnastic pad, and he shot his load one last time. That was the perfect ending to a perfect night. We were both huffing and puffing. He said, "I can see how someone could have a heart attack exerting themselves like this."

"Glad we're in such good shape." I finished his sentence for him.

"You are incredible!" we both said at the same time.

"You know what would be nice? Going back over to your place and washing up. And since you're such a good cook you can rustle us up some vittles," I said in a fake southern drawl.

"Yes, it would, milady, except we'd probably wake up my wife. And that wouldn't be a good thing to do," he said.

"Your wife? What the fuck!" I screamed. "I'm no homewrecker!"

"No, you're not; there's no home to wreck," he said. "When you saw me at that light by the railroad tracks, I had just left home to go to work at the airport. My wife said goodbye to me by telling me that I should be glad to have her because no one else would want me. And then you came along like an angel from Heaven. You wanted me! How could I say no to that? I'm sorry I lied, but did I really?"

He asked me in such a pleading way. But I had to stay resolute—I was not going to cave in to my feelings for him, great sex or no great sex.

"Yes, you lied to me just to get a piece of ass. I hoped you liked it because the train stops here and now. Sorry about your situation at home, but that's your problem, not mine. Get a divorce and come find me in Miami. I can't believe this bullshit! But until that happens I don't want to see you or hear from you. Do you understand me?" I said, holding back my tears.

So Miami it was, ASAP! Men in Philly are just jerks! Hasta la vista, baby!

Chapter 2

HICKORY SWITCH

ONE OF MY FAVORITE POSITIONS is a pretty tame one, but, when done at the right time and place, it will lead to a mind-numbing orgasm for both him and her. It's called the "hickory switch," but it only sounds painful. As with any position, passion is always the key. Like the song says, you live or die for … passion! Thank you, Rod Stewart, for those words of wisdom.

Whether you're on your back or face down with your ass way up in the air, the hickory switch remains the same. If you're on your knees, your lover can add more stimuli by playing with your asshole with his thumb. Yes, the bigger the thumb, the more intense the pleasure. Troy Aikman—Hall of Fame, Dallas Cowboy, and Super Bowl quarterback—has the biggest set of thumbs I have ever seen. I get so wet when he broadcasts a football game, like every other woman in America does, that it sends shivers through my body. Hey, how about them Cowboys, right, girls?

Anyway, back to the hickory switch. My lover enters

me and sets up a good rhythm; I can play with my clit while he's pumping away inside me. So picture this: I'm on my knees while my lover is deep inside me with his thumb in my tight asshole; my fingers are strumming my clit. His other hand is on my waist while I suck his big toe, so he goes deeper inside me. When he gets close to cumming I pop off of his dick and lie on my back, my knees thrown back to my shoulders, and let him use his erect penis to spank my throbbing clit. This sends jolts of electricity through my body and his. He then jams his cock back into my sopping pussy to build up the pressure and momentum again (you can repeat this process again and again—if you're lucky).

When he can't take it anymore and finally cums (very deep inside me), he saves some of his spunk for that hickory switch of his and slaps me across the face with his penis. Upon his orgasm, he lets loose with the final pumps of hot cream that go down the back of my throat.

Yummy, yummy, yummy, I got his love in my tummy. That should be a song!

Chapter 3

FORKS IN THE ROAD

THERE'S AN OLD SAYING: WHEN you come to a fork in the road, you should always take the fork. This is a little story of that fork being taken.

I love sex. Sex with your lover should be a no-holds-barred, carnal wrestling match where you both win. Nothing should be off the table. If he wants a blow job and you want to give him one, there is nothing wrong with giving him a blow job. Believe me, I really want my lover to go down on me.

Where does it say in the Bible that blow jobs or eating pussy is wrong? It doesn't. Where does it say in the Bible that anal sex between a man and woman is wrong? It doesn't. Anything between two consenting adults is okay. So, if this was a sin, I'm pretty sure God would tell us very plainly, "Hey, that's a sin!" which he didn't do.

One of my best times, top ten for sure, was when a lover came over, and from that first kiss at the door it was on. He started kissing my mouth and my neck, and then my clothes just vanished off me. His tongue was magic as he dropped to his knees and started licking my clit—very roughly and then oh, so softly. He went back and forth, and it drove me right up the wall. Then he maneuvered me over to the couch, pushed me onto my back, and entered me in one fell swoop. The heat between us was incredible; he was trying to overload my sexual senses. One of his hands squeezed my breast and the other hand strummed my clit, while he nibbled my neck and pounded my pussy.

Then he threw my knees back to my shoulders and removed his engorged cock from my pussy. He said, "What do we have here?" as he found my tight little asshole.

I breathed deep, *Oh my gosh, oh my gosh, oh my gosh!* I thought as I panted, "Easy, lover."

The head of his cock was so big! His cock was so lubricated by my juices that it didn't hurt as he stuck the head in my asshole. Then he pulled out and slammed it back in my pussy; with the next stroke he entered my asshole. Back and forth this went as he built up a good rhythm. Sweat was pouring out of him as he said, "I'm about to cum, baby. Where do you want me to?"

"Anywhere and everywhere, baby," I panted, as I must have cum a dozen times already. His hands were on my hips as he was alternating between my pussy and asshole with every stroke.

"Here it cums, baby!"

We both screamed a very primal, carnal scream that turned into a long, exhausting but satisfying moan as we came and collapsed in a heaping mound of sweaty sex.

BLOODY BUFFET

I LOVE ORAL SEX, BOTH GIVING and receiving. I love to eat pussy and suck some hard cock, but most of all I love to have my pussy eaten, especially when I'm on my period. Nothing gets my juices flowing like having my lover go down on me during my cycle. I remember the first time I experienced an orgasm this way. It was mind blowing. I was actually late for my period the first time it happened. It wasn't like it was the first time I was late, so I wasn't panicking … yet.

My Cuban lover would meet me at my place after my last class, and instead of going out to eat, we usually dined in. He had such a ravenous appetite for me. He treated me like a buffet. The lights were always on—I mean, he wanted to see what he was eating. He would suck on my clit, very softly at first, then would lick with more pressure in each stroke. Then he would insert two fingers into my sopping pussy and one into my very tight asshole. It was like sensory overload to the nth degree. All the while I would put my hand on his head, pushing him deeper into my pussy. He would always tell me how great I tasted and how he wanted more and more of me.

On this particular day, he got the more he wanted. After he made me explode a few times, he came up for air; we were both out of breath from him making me cum hard multiple times. That's when I burst out laughing. He asked, "What's so funny?" I told him not to be mad at me but to go look in the mirror. He was shocked, to say the least.

My period had started during one of my orgasms, and when I exploded, I exploded all over his face. The corners of his pencil thin mustache were caked in my blood. He looked like an insane clown. At first he was as shocked as I was, but then he started laughing—like an insane clown! I started laughing as well. I saw we had ruined a nice set of sheets, but that was just a small price to pay for all those wonderful orgasms he had given me.

He said he couldn't really tell the difference in my pussy taste when I was on my period or off—he loved it either way. I sure as hell didn't mind. I was getting my pussy eaten no matter when. Talk about a win-win. Dinner is now served 365 days or nights of the year. The buffet is always open for him. Yummy, yummy, yummy, he's got my love in his tummy now.

Chapter 5

ITALIAN MUSTACHE

SEX SHOULD BE FUN. IT should be silly as well. You need to enjoy all aspects of what you are doing. If you don't, then why do it at all? We call this activity the "Italian mustache." This is the silliest thing I've ever done—hope you enjoy it as much as I did.

You get your lover to trim his or her pubes. You can even cut the pubes up so they are that much finer. Put said pubes in a plastic bag and then do what comes natural (this means, fuck your brains out).

When he is about to cum, he disengages from you and whacks off onto your face. Now make sure he does not erupt into your mouth. Or better yet, just keep your mouth closed while he cums all over your face. I always have a hard time with this because I'm such a cum-a-holic.

So anyway, he blasts his hot sticky cum all over your face. Then he reaches for the bag of cut pubes and releases them—all over your face. Voilà, instant mustache and goatee. And to make this Italian, you yell out, "Now, that's a spicy meatball!"

Chapter 6

BICYCLE BRIDGE FOR TWO

H AVE YOU EVER ENJOYED FUCKING around where you might get caught? You know what could happen, right? On the down side, yes, you could go to jail. But on the up side you could make memories to last a lifetime, and isn't that what's life all about? Pity the poor fools that have no memories to look back on with a smile. This is one of those times. I didn't go to jail, but I almost got caught. It was very thrilling, and I recommend you try this.

My lover and I were in a playful mood, but we didn't want to play at home. I told him it was such a beautiful night out we should make love under the stars. We were driving on a highway within city limits, and we passed under one of those bicycle bridges built so that children can go to school safely. That gave me a great idea. I told my lover to pull off at the next exit. He had no idea what I had in mind.

As we got out of the car and walked toward the middle of the bridge, I told him to be on the lookout for the police. The cars were speeding past us down below as I dropped to my knees and unzipped his pants.

He exclaimed, "What are you doing?"

I said, "You know what I'm doing, baby. It's not like they can stop and watch us, so just enjoy! Be on the lookout for joggers or the police."

I didn't have to wait long for the desired results. I stood up, shimmied out of my one-piece dress, and told him to go at it. That's exactly what he did—he grabbed me by the hips as I extended my arms and grabbed the fence. My breasts were caught between the hexagon shapes of the fence as he rammed me against it, leaving the indention of the fence on my breasts. Down below, the traffic was speeding past us at over seventy miles an hour, and they only got a glimpse of the action. Some saw enough to honk at us, but there was no way they could stop or turn around. The surge of adrenaline was upon us both, and we put on quite the show for the cars beneath us.

He pumped his hot seed into me, and there was so much that it leaked down my leg. I must have cum every time a car honked. He was getting his, and I was sure getting mine.

Right then we saw the headlights of a car approaching where our car was parked. So we got back into our clothes and walked away from the center of the bridge looking like two lovers enjoying a midnight summer stroll. We waved at the car as it drove past us, and we got back into our car, all smiles I might add. We had made a great memory that would last forever.

Chapter 7

LIGHTS ... CAMERA ... ACTION!

ONE OF MY MOST MEMORABLE times was when me and my guy went to see the latest Marvel movie for the fourth or fifth time. If you've never had sex in a movie theater, I suggest you do it. Find a theater with big cushy lounge chairs that recline all the way back. Make sure you've seen the movie before so you don't get caught up in it and forget your partner.

We were in the very top row, so no one could see what we were about to do, and luckily no one else was in the row with us. I unzipped his fly and released the "dragon of love" as he called it. My gosh, his dragon was raring to go! So big and so thick, like I'd never seen it before. I couldn't wait to get my tongue on it. I gobbled him up, while at the same time fingering myself.

Then I couldn't take it any longer. I raised my skirt up and climbed onto him, impaling myself on him. I had to remind myself not to cry out so no one would notice us. Thank goodness those Marvel movies are so loud. I worked up a good rhythm while his big strong hands held onto my hips. I started riding him slow, then got gradually faster. He grabbed my hair with one hand as he pinched my nipples with his other. By the time he was ready to cum, I was a bronco busting high in the saddle.

He moaned that he was ready to cum, while slipping his fingers around me to strum my engorged clit. Talk about lights out, my head was spinning like a top! The fight scene was about to hit its climax on the big screen and so were we! I wasn't sure if any of the other patrons heard us, and I really didn't care.

Wow, he was so deep inside me that when he finally let loose it was earth-shattering. Three, four, five hot squirts of jizz shot up into my hungry pussy. We just stayed frozen there for a few minutes basking in the afterglow of our sex. We could feel our juices trickle out of my sopping cunt past his lap and onto the fake leather upholstery. The air around us was pungent with our sex smell. Thank goodness there were a good twenty seats between us and the next closest people.

I put my arm around his head and pulled him close to me twisting to kiss him. I told him, there was more where that came from when we get home, and oh boy, was there!

Chapter 8

CAUGHT ON CAMERA

EVER HAD TO USE AN ATM to get money? Yes, you have—everybody has. It's quick and easy—just like I am with my man.

One night we're looking for a place to eat and he says he needs to get some cash. As he jumps out of the car heading for the ATM door, I notice how hot he looks—with his broad shoulders and his cascading blonde hair that bounces with every step.

I look around and see no one, so I jump out of the car as well. I say to him, "Hey, big boy, what's a nice guy like you doing in a place like this?"

As I saunter over to him, placing my thumb over the little camera hole, I say, "Nobody can see us now. Put your thumb where mine is, so we can have a little fun."

I drop to my knees while reaching up to unzip his pants so we can release his penis, and boy, was it ready to be released.

He says, "Hope there's no one watching the camera feeds because we'll be on the nightly news, I bet." I tell him that these are just security cameras, and the tapes are only viewed when someone needs to check a specific period of time. Anyway, with his thumb over the camera there will be nothing to see.

Back to the moment at hand—I start to gobble him up. He lets out a small moan as both of his hands go around the back of my head. He starts to buck wildly as he fucks my face with a ferociousness I have never seen from him. The sound echoes in the small cramped space as he lets out a guttural roar of conquest. As he continues to fuck my face I slide my index finger up his ass to prod him on. I want my salty reward before we get caught. Large streams of drool are hanging from my mouth and from his cock. I try to slurp as much of the stuff back in my ravenous mouth.

"I'm about to cum," he moans as he pulls his engorged member from my mouth and places his cock on the tip of my tongue.

"Come on baby," I coax him. "Mommy is hungry— give me, give me, give me," as I continue to finger fuck his ass.

All of a sudden he tenses up and there is that sweet, salty release I've been craving. Large strips of cum paint the side of my face and spurt in my mouth as I hungrily try to catch as much of it as I can. I ease my finger from his ass and show him how hungry I am for every essence of him by raking my finger through his cum and sucking it down my throat.

I say with a smile, "Fantastic appetizer, now let's find a place for the main course."

He replies, "Beef: it's what's for dinner," and we both laugh.

Chapter 9

DRIVE-BY DRILLING

ONE OF THE BEST TIMES I've ever had was in my lover's car, and, since it was a two-seater, I don't mean the back seat.

It started out when my boyfriend picked me up at the end of a long work day for an evening out on the town. He kissed me, and he smelled so good that it just sent me out of this world. I started playfully rubbing my hands all over my man's sexy, hairy chest and tweaking his nipples. While my hands were on him, his hand was on me. Talk about multi-tasking! I don't know how he could keep control of the car and me at the same time. We pulled out onto the busiest street in town, but I didn't care—I wanted my man. I was so horny and wet, practically drenched in my love juices, due to his adept middle finger that "rocked my little man in the boat."

As he expertly maneuvered through rush-hour traffic, I just as expertly maneuvered my head onto his cock while he finger fucked me to orgasm. I love the taste of my man, but I was too far gone; I told him I was going to fuck him right then and there and didn't give two shits who knew what was going on.

I shimmied out of my sopping wet thong and straddled my boyfriend. Since he was so tall, he had the seat pushed all the way back; it was a tight but pretty good fit. I lowered myself onto his cock and let him completely fill up my sex-starved pussy. We stopped at traffic lights, drove through traffic like it wasn't there, and had just the most wonderful fuck you can imagine. Did people know what we were doing? I didn't know and didn't care. All I knew was it was a great fuck.

He told me he was about to cum, so I hopped off of him and gobbled his dick with a lightning quick reaction. I slurped on his big thick dick, long and hard like the sex-starved wench I was, until I got my salty prize.

When I came up for air, I noticed we were in a traffic jam, and there was this beautiful redheaded lady in a Ford pick'em up truck applauding the little show we had put on. I gave her a sheepishly big grin and stuck out my cum-coated tongue at her, which I cleaned with a good raking from my front teeth. Then I swallowed the excess cum as she motioned for us to follow her into the next parking lot.

We pulled over, and the longest set of freckled legs that I had ever seen eased from her king cab. Me and my man both said, "Wow," at the same time.

She slowly walked over to my side of the car as both our heads swayed to her hips swishing back and forth in perfect rhythm. *I have to learn how to walk like that*, I thought.

"How does two redheads for the price of one sound to you, honey?"

"Damn skippy!" my boyfriend replied.

She squatted down like a baseball catcher beside my car door and asked in a gravelly voice, "He really does have a big dick, doesn't he?"

I was still holding onto his nice hunk of man meat, which was shrinking as fast as it could, nodding my head in the affirmative as I tried to show it off to her.

"Honey, this girl is a guy," my man said.

"No shit, Sherlock," the girl, no the guy, with the stunning legs said.

Well, now I understood why his Mr. Happy wasn't so happy anymore.

"Wow, you are really beautiful!" I told her, "But what happens when they find out you have a dick instead of a pussy?"

She replied, "Honey, I paid $30,000 for this pussy. I have a pussy—or an expertly quaffed v-jay jay as some would call it. And after I get my vocal cords worked on next month, I will be all woman. How would you like to get together then?" she asked as she slipped me her business card. "I bet we could have a really good time."

To which my man said, "Sorry darling, I don't do guys. Even if they become girls, just not my thing." He took her card out of my hand and handed it back to her. "Take care and good luck," he said, starting up the engine and pulling away as I was waving goodbye to her ... him ... soon to be her? I dunno.

"Didn't see that coming when those legs slid out of the truck," my boyfriend said as we both laughed and went on with our evening.

Chapter 10

GOLDEN HERSHEY HIGHWAY: MY WAY, THE RIGHT WAY, THE ONLY WAY

END THIS BOOK WITH THE wildest sexual adventure I have had to date. This one has it all, but most of all, it has passion. Passion in the most important ingredient there is when it comes to lovemaking. If you don't have passion it just becomes copulating, and that's what animals do. Like the song says, you have to live or die for … passion!

A former lover of mine was transferring to a small town outside of Chattanooga, Tennessee, and he said he wanted to make our last night something I would never forget. So we had a fantastic dinner, and then we went back to his place.

We started kissing and touching and rubbing as I unzipped his pants, and right on cue his penis was bobbing in front of my face. There was a string of pre-cum that stretched from his cock to my mouth. I inhaled him and, as if on cue, he groaned as I took as much of him as I could. His hands slipped behind my head and he told me to ease up. He didn't want to explode too early—not tonight.

We made love in every position imaginable—me on top, then him on top, then on my knees, belly, and even me upside down with most of my weight on my shoulders. That was an awesome position because he was pistoning his cock into my pussy and then my asshole like a machine. He was relentless. Over and over he plunged in and out of my wet, squirting pussy and sloppy asshole. Finally, he said the magic words, "I'm about to explode," and he grabbed my hips and pulled me even closer to him.

"Do it, baby," I moaned. And then I felt those streaks of hot cum shooting into my gaping pussy. "My legs are dead, but keep giving it to me, honey," I moaned in intense pleasure.

"Oh, I'm not done yet, baby!" His cock swelled up inside my pussy as he alternated between my asshole and my cunt. He was driving me crazy, just pumping away, fucking me with reckless abandon. Was he going to give me a second load that would spurt out of my cunt or asshole and onto my belly and bed, or was this the third load knowing my pussy couldn't hold much more of his hot creamy load? "Here it comes, baby!"

Then the most incredible feeling encompassed me. It wasn't just a spurt, spurt here and a spurt, spurt there; this was like a fucking fire hose spraying full blast into my pussy. He didn't miss a beat as he expertly went back and forth from my pussy to my greedy asshole. It was incredible, as I came countless times!

It was the hottest enema I ever experienced. "I didn't think a guy could piss with a hard-on?" I said, my voice still shaky from the intense orgasms I had just experienced.

"It takes a bit of practice, darling. Did you like?" He asked, knowing full well I did. "I learned, from the internet, pee is sterile and you won't catch any disease from having it on you or inside you."

"Wrong, baby," I said. "Nothing about the human body is sterile. I just need to go douche real good and get myself super clean. That means, since this is your place, you get to clean up this mess. See you in a few, babe."

After I cleaned myself up I came back to his arms, and we made love one last time. No competition, no rushing to see who could get each other off the fastest. Just sweet lovemaking like it's supposed to be made.

We said our goodbyes the next morning, and we each went on our separate ways; maybe we would see each other again if the opportunity presented itself.

Epilogue

There you have it. All the memories are true, in exact detail, just the names have been changed to protect those that might think they are innocent. Ha! Innocence— that's something that can never be reclaimed once lost.

Hoped you learned a lot about lovemaking and passion. Sex is never wrong between two consenting adults. God didn't create all these sexy men and women so we would ban ourselves from enjoying each other. Sex sustains us, it recharges us for the next day, hour, or just for the next whatever.

You need to protect yourself. If that means getting checked out by a doctor, then get yourself checked out by a doctor. Make sure you use protection if need be because no one else will ever protect you like you will protect yourself.

You should never be ashamed of your sex life. You should never box yourself into a corner because a potential partner is overweight. Fat guys have big dicks, just like fat chicks have tight pussies. It's all about finding that right formula for the passion you want and need. If you want to date outside your race, then go for it! If you connect with someone on a spiritual, physical, and emotional level then their race should be the least important thing about them.

This has not been a work of fiction, no matter what the disclaimer said. Every story was true. What do I want you to do? Go write your own story, and have fun doing it!

If this book does well, my next book might blow away the political landscape of this country we live in. My next book will be called, *My Affair with the President.*

J. K. Meyers will return soon—but not soon enough.

Printed in Great Britain
by Amazon